O9-BRZ-690

Date: 7/22/11

E TIMMERS
Timmers, Leo.
Who is driving? /

PALM BEACH COUNTY
LIBRARY SYSTEM
3650 Summit Boulevard
West Palm Beach, FL 33406-4198

Who Is Driving?

Leo Timmers

BLOOMSBURY
CHILDREN'S
BOOKS

Who is driving…

...the fire engine?

Elephant!

He is driving to the fire station.

*wee*ooo*h wee*ooo*h wee*ooo*h*

Who is driving...

...the fancy car?

Cat!

She is driving to a tea party.

zzzzZOOMmmm

Who is driving…

...the race car?

Rabbit!

He is driving to the racetrack.

vrooooooomm

Who is driving…

...the tractor?

Pig!

He is driving to the farm.

_{putt} *putt* *putt* *putt* *putt*

Who is driving...

...the convertible?

Giraffe!

She is driving to the tennis courts.

brom **brom** *brom* **brom** *brom* **brom**

Who is driving…

...the jeep?

Hippopotamus!

He is driving to the jungle.

takke takke takke **tak**

Who is flying...

...the airplane?

Stork!

She is flying to Paris.

whooooooossshh

But who...

...will get there first?

Copyright © 2005 by Leo Timmers
Translation copyright © 2007 by Clavis Uitgeverij
First published in Belgium in 2005 as *Wie Rijdt?* by Clavis Uitgeverij

All rights reserved. No part of this book may be used or reproduced
in any manner whatsoever without written permission from the publisher,
except in the case of brief quotations embodied in critical articles or reviews.

Typeset in Bodoni
Art created with acrylic paints

Published by Bloomsbury Publishing, New York, London, and Berlin
Distributed to the trade by Holtzbrinck Publishers

Library of Congress Cataloging-in-Publication Data
Timmers, Leo.
[Wie rijdt? English]
Who is driving? / by Leo Timmers. — 1st U.S. ed.
p.   cm.
Summary: Easy-to-read text invites the reader to guess which animal is driving each of seven
vehicles based on how they are dressed, then reveals their destinations and the vehicles' sounds.
ISBN-10: 1-59990-021-1 • ISBN-13: 978-1-59990-021-6
[1. Vehicles—Fiction. 2. Animals—Fiction. 3. Sounds, Words for—Fiction.] I. Title.
PZ7.T4862Who 2007   [E]—dc22   2006009541

First U.S. Edition 2007
Printed in China
3 5 7 9 10 8 6 4

Bloomsbury Publishing, Children's Books, U.S.A.
175 Fifth Avenue, New York, NY 10010